More Monsters, More Problems

Adapted by Tracey West

SCHOLASTIC INC.

ISBN: 978-1-338-03804-0

10 9 8 7 6 5 4 3 2 1   16 17 18 19 20

Printed in the U.S.A. 40

First printing 2016

Book design by Rick DeMonico

CONTENTS

The kingdom of Knighton used to be a happy, peaceful place. But the castle held a dark secret—The Book of Monsters.

A long time ago, an evil wizard named Monstrox unleashed monsters on Knighton. A good wizard, Merlok, trapped the monsters in one book—The Book of Monsters—and kept them locked away for decades.

Then one day the power went out, and Jestro, the unhappy court jester, found The Book of Monsters. The talking book convinced Jestro to turn against King Halbert and bring the monsters within his pages to life.

How do you save a kingdom from an army of Lava Monsters? That's where the NEXO KNIGHTS team came in! Clay, Macy, Lance, Aaron, and Axl were able to fight the monsters with powers downloaded from Merlok's new digital form, Merlok 2.0.

So far, they've kept The Book of Monsters and Jestro from taking over Knighton. But bigger, badder monsters are coming to life every day! Can the NEXO KNIGHTS heroes keep their kingdom from plunging into darkness?

CHAPTER 1

The tall castle rose up from jagged rocks, bubbling, hot lava pits, and steaming sulfur pools. Two large, curved horns sat on top of the tallest turret. They looked sinister against the dark, red sky.

Inside his Redoubt of Ruination, Jestro the Jester laughed. His cackle bounced off the stone walls.

"I am the king of my own castle!" he crowed. "How great is that?"

Jestro didn't look like a king at all. He still wore his blue-and-red jester costume. It was jagged and dirty from battle. His yellow, evil eyes looked strange against his pale white jester makeup. In his right hand, he carried a scepter topped with a spiked circle. Its magic could bring monsters to life from the pages of The Book of Monsters.

The Bookkeeper, the little red monster who carried around The Book of Monsters, brought the book closer to Jestro's throne.

"You're right it's great," agreed The Book of Monsters. "No more trying to grab that shiny house King Halbert's got. Now we got the castle of Monstrox himself! This place is much homier."

Jestro looked around from his perch on his rock-carved throne. There wasn't much other furniture in the spooky castle. Two monsters—Burnzie and Sparkks—were busy moving around a stone table and chairs.

"Yeah, it is pretty homey," said Jestro. "It's very, uh, rustic."

The Book of Monsters gasped. "I hope by rustic you don't mean horrible and decrepit?" he asked.

"No!" Jestro replied. "I mean, you know, naturalistic and with more of an earthy vibe."

Then Jestro sighed. "I'm just, not sure what to do next," he said. "I'm not really a 'homebody,' you know?"

"Totally get it," The Book of Monsters said. "And castle maintenance can be so boring."

Clunk! As he said it, Burnzie and Sparkks bumped into each other. They both tumbled onto the hard castle floor.

The Book of Monsters rolled his eyes. Those two magma monsters were great in battle, but they were terrible movers!

"Besides," Jestro continued. "Every castle needs a big chamber filled with treasure. That means we better get out there and do some major looting."

"I know a guy who would be perfect for the job," said The Book of Monsters. "General Magmar. He was Monstrox's right-hand man. Take-charge kinda guy."

Jestro looked interested. "A general, eh?"

"The best," the book assured him. "Check page thirty-eight."

Each page of The Book of Monsters contained monsters trapped inside by magic. The Bookkeeper opened the book to page thirty-eight. Jestro smiled when he saw the picture of General Magmar.

Jestro raised his wand and quickly thought up a rhyme to bring General Magmar out of the book.

"I want to go looting wide and far. So come on out, General Magmar!"

As he spoke, a magical, glowing purple-and-gold light shone inside the spiked circle on top of his wand. The page of the book started to glow, too.

Boom! The light exploded and created a huge cloud in front of Jestro. When it faded, a monster stood before him.

General Magmar had a red body like the other Lava Monsters. He was slightly taller than Jestro, and the black ponytail that sprouted from the top of his head made him look even taller. He wore armor just around his mouth, exposing his eyes. Around his waist, he wore a black belt that bore the symbol of the evil jester.

The general bowed to Jestro. "I am at your command, oh evil one," he said in a deep voice.

"Wow, you seem to have a lava brain in that monster head," Jestro said. He looked at The Book of Monsters. "He makes a great first impression!"

"Hmm," said General Magmar, sizing up his new commander.

Jestro turned back to the monster. "Okay, you're a general. So I want you to be general manager of castle operations. Now, you make this place deadly for anyone who tries to sneak in, and we'll go out pillaging and looting the countryside."

"What?" cried The Book of Monsters. "Have you lost your pointy-hatted mind? He's a hardened battle leader!"

General Magmar cleared his throat. "Sir, maybe you didn't hear him. I have studied strategy, battle tactics . . ."

"So you can add some nice, tactical-ish traps to make this place more homey!" Jestro said cheerfully.

"Unacceptable!" shrieked The Book of Monsters. "I demand that you . . ."

"And I demand that you shut your cover, encyclo-dopia! I'm in charge!" Jestro fumed.

He looked at the general. "Now, General Manager, start, um, fixing."

General Magmar's yellow eyes glared at Jestro. "I am at your command," he said. Then he lowered his voice. "Even though you are completely wasting my time."

"What?" Jestro asked.

"I said, 'Have a wonderful time!'" General Magmar lied.

Then he walked off, leaving Jestro to go off looting and pillaging.

CHAPTER 2

Bang! Clash! Slam!

Sounds of battle practice echoed from the Fortrex—the blue castle on wheels belonging to the heroes. They lived there, trained there, and were ready at a moment's notice to defend the kingdom against Jestro and The Book of Monsters.

"Aargh!" grunted Macy as she fended off a blow from a sword with her shield.

Her opponent was Robin Underwood, a freshman at Knights' Academy. Wearing a pair of mechanical stilts, he towered over Macy.

"Hah!" cried Macy as she swung her mace at Robin.

Wham! She whacked at one of the stilts with all her might.

"Whoa!" Robin yelled as he toppled over backward. He sat up, rubbing his head.

"Good job!" Macy complimented him. "But tell me, Robin—why are you here? Lance is on the schedule."

Macy didn't mind training with Robin. But she was a real knight, and he still had a lot to learn. Training with Robin was more like teaching, when what Macy wanted was a real workout that would truly test her skills as a knight.

"He paid me to take his training spot," Robin replied.

"Does he think he can buy his way out of anything?" Macy asked angrily.

Robin shrugged. "Uh, pretty much!"

At that very moment, Lance was reclining in a chair in the Fortrex lounge. His golden-blond hair fell in perfect waves across his forehead. His white armor gleamed, thanks to the work of his personal Squirebot, Dennis. His chest bore the symbol of a white horse, the crest of the Richmond family.

Across from him sat Ava Prentis, another freshman at Knights' Academy and a tech whiz of major proportions. She was busy tapping away on the screen of a gold cell phone.

"Oh, and make my background photo that picture of me at the latest Holo-Wood premiere," Lance was saying. "I looked great!"

"Whatevs," said Ava in a bored voice. "You're paying me to program this thing."

She pulled up a photo of Lance grinning at the camera with a dazzling smile.

"I am going to have the greatest phone ever!" Lance cheered. "That is, until the new version comes out in six months, right?"

"Very trendy," said Ava in her usual flat voice. "But I'm not an early adopter."

"What's the difference?" Lance asked. "I

want to make sure it's ready for the B-I-G party tonight at my parents' house."

Macy stormed into the lounge. Without her helmet, her dark red hair stuck up from the top of her head in a ponytail.

"Lance, what's the big idea of paying Robin to take your spot on the training schedule?" she asked.

"I had more important things to do," Lance replied.

"Yeah, I can see," Macy said sarcastically, pointing to the couch Lance was on. Then she got angry. "Look, I may be a princess, but I want to be treated like a normal person. You're a rich kid who wants to remind everyone how special you are."

"Talk to Axl. I'm paying him to handle all complaints," Lance said, pointing to the big-screen video game system nearby. Big, muscular team member Axl sat on the couch, playing a game called "Whackman & the

Super Mega Power Panic" and munching on a giant turkey leg.

"Ohhhh!" Macy cried, exasperated. She turned and stomped out of the lounge.

Lance turned to Ava. "Now, let's pick an awesome ring tone . . ."

CHAPTER 3

Jestro and The Book of Monsters (carried by the Bookkeeper) roamed the countryside of Knighton.

On the day that Jestro first found The Book of Monsters, they battled with Merlok in the wizard's library. The fight ended with a big explosion, and the evil books were scattered around the kingdom. Jestro and The Book of Monsters had found some of them, but there were still more to find.

Now The Book of Monsters sniffed the air. That's how he found the missing books—he could smell the evil!

"Hey, I smell something!" the book said, excited. "This way!"

The Bookkeeper carried him toward the smell, and Jestro followed. They entered a dark cave.

Inside the cave, a book with a red cover was lodged into a crack in a big rock. The image of a gold gem glittered on the cover. The pages glittered with gold, too. Jestro's eyes lit up.

"Wow! What a find!" said The Book of Monsters. "The Book of Greed. You want dungeons filled with treasure? Well, you just hit the jackpot, Juggle Boy!"

"Oh yes!" Jestro cheered. "I bet this will let me make greedy monsters that will fill my new castle with gold and jewels and . . . more gold!"

The Book of Monsters' eyes glowed with fiery evil.

"Greed," he said. "Greed is good!"

"And I know the best place to get all the booty we want," said Jestro. "The richest town in the kingdom . . . Auremville!"

CHAPTER 4

The road to Auremville was paved with real gold. It wound past houses made of gold, protected by fences made of gold. Streetlights made of gold cast a golden glow on the golden sidewalks at night. During the day, armies of Squirebots polished all the gold until it gleamed so brightly you needed sunglasses to look at it.

On this bright, sunny day, four vehicles zoomed along the golden road. Lance led the way in his Turbo Jouster, followed by Macy's Thunder Mace, Axl's Tower Carrier, and Clay's Rumble Blade. Aaron had hitched a ride in Axl's tank.

They came to a stop at the golden gates

of the Richmond Estate, a huge golden mansion. Tall bushes sculpted into the shape of giant horse heads lined the grounds.

Lance hopped out of his vehicle followed by his pet pig, Hamletta. A Squirebot in a butler's uniform waited for them, holding a golden cloth.

Lance wiped his hands on the cloth while another Squirebot started to polish the pig.

"Hmm," said Lance, looking around. "Looks like Mom and Dad wanted to have a small party this year. How boring. Right, Hamletta?"

"Oink!" replied the cute pink pig.

"Just one family lives here?" asked Axl in disbelief. "It's bigger than my whole town."

The knights followed Lance inside to a huge entrance hallway. Food was piled onto tables, and Squirebots carrying golden goblets walked around, handing beverages to the Richmonds' guests.

"Quite the spread you got here, Lance," remarked Clay, the knights' leader.

“This is like the party scene from the *Ned Knightly: On the King’s Secret Service* movie,” Macy said. “Is *everything* gold?”

“Well, the water in the lake out back isn’t gold,” Lance replied. “But it’s filled with goldfish.”

Macy rolled her eyes. “Oh, brother!”

“Ah, the NEXO KNIGHTS team!” a voice interrupted them.

It was Lance’s father, Cuthbert. He and his wife, Goldie, walked up to the knights. They both wore fancy white clothing stitched with gold thread. Each wore the symbol of the Richmond family, the horse head.

“Welcome to our annual ‘Gold Is Good’ ball,” Goldie greeted them.

“Mom? Dad? The party this year seems . . . tiny,” Lance said.

“We booked a spa holiday that starts tomorrow, and we didn’t want the servants to have too much cleaning up to do,” his mother explained.

"Isn't that their job?" Lance asked.

"Oh, son. Eat some gold ice cream and try not to be such a disappointment," Goldie said, leading him away.

Cuthbert walked up to Clay.

"Why, you must be Mr. Moorington," he said. "I do so enjoy your swordplay. Come, let me show you my weapons collection."

"I'd be honored, sir," Clay replied politely.

The huge Fortrex pulled up outside the mansion gates and screeched to a stop. The vehicle's drawbridge opened and Robin and Ava walked out.

Robin looked excited. "Whoa, this is going to be some party!"

Ava handed the keys to the Fortrex to the Squirebot valet parker.

"The clutch is a little tricky," she said. "And wash and wax it by the time we get back."

The Squirebot looked up at the giant vehicle and gulped. Life was pretty sweet in the Land of Gold—unless you were a Squirebot!

CHAPTER 5

Jestro's Evil Mobile pulled up to the village of Buttonburg in Knighton. His favorite monsters, Burnzie and Sparkks, pulled the vehicle with glowing lava chains. The front of the Evil Mobile looked like a monster face with a jester's cap, glowing orange eyes, and mouth filled with sharp teeth. Jestro and The Book of Monsters stood on the very top.

Jestro had decided to make a stop before hitting Auremville. Buttonburg made all of the buttons in Knighton. A blue hologram of a button glowed on top of the town's tallest tower.

"I wanna make sure this greedy book

works before we hit Auremville," Jestro said, examining the book in his hands.

He shoved it inside The Book of Monsters' mouth. The book eagerly gobbled it up, his eyes glowing with excitement. Every time he ate a new evil book, the monsters appeared on his pages.

"Oh, that is so tasty," he said. "It's like potato chips. I just want more, more, more!"

Jestro opened the book to the pages containing the new monsters.

"Greedy, greedy monsters, come out and steal some stuff!" he chanted. "Loot and loot and plunder. You can never have enough!"

A cloud of purple magic exploded from the book, and a small army of monsters rained down in front of the Evil Mobile.

Round, red Globlins bounced up and down, anxious to do some evil. Red Scurriers, short creatures with stubby arms and legs, cackled with glee. Spider Globlins tapped their spiderlike legs impatiently on the road.

Burnzie laughed. The mammoth monster had yellow eyes, wicked horns, and a red body that looked like it had been carved from a volcano.

"Grab anything gold! Or jeweled!" he yelled.

Next to him Sparkks was itching to loot and pillage. The monster's body looked like it had been chiseled from black rock. He had one huge, glowing, yellow eye in the middle of his face.

"Treasure! I want treasure!" he cried.

The monsters stormed into the village. The peaceful citizens gasped in fright when they saw the evil army.

The monsters laughed at the frightened villagers. They burst into shops and houses, stealing crates, trunks, and barrels of buttons. One by one, they returned to the Evil Mobile with their loot.

Jestro was pleased. "Oh, they are greedy, looting monster machines!" he cheered. The red dots in his eyes started to twirl like pinwheels.

"Oh yeah!" agreed The Book of Monsters. "Just think how they'll be when they hit a town filled with gold!"

"Auremville even has gold toilets," Jestro said.

"And gold toilet paper!" said the book. He laughed, and his long, red tongue snaked out of his mouth. "Let's take every last golden bit of it!"

CHAPTER 6

Back at the Richmond mansion, the guests were having a great time. They ate fancy food and listened to Squirebot musicians playing classical music.

Clay stepped out onto the terrace overlooking the city. Axl joined him, holding a gold turkey drumstick.

"Lance's father has quite the collection of weapons," Clay remarked. "All gold, of course."

"And the food!" Axl said, impressed. "This drumstick is actually basted in gold."

"What does gold taste like?" Clay asked.

He heard Lance's voice answer behind him.

"Like coming home . . ."

Clay turned to see Lance in a gold chair, carried by four Squirebot butlers. Two more Squirebots carried Hamletta in on a smaller chair. They set them both down and began to polish Lance's armor—and Hamletta—with gold cloths.

"Being surrounded by people to serve me is so refreshing," Lance said with a satisfied sigh.

Freckle-faced, ginger-haired Aaron Fox came flying onto the terrace, riding his hover shield. He landed on the edge of the terrace and kick-flipped the shield into his hand.

"Lance, buddy, that golden hover board park you got out back is the bomb!" he told his friend.

"Are you talking about the small one near the golf course or the big one near the stable filled with golden unicorns?" Lance wanted to know.

Before Aaron could answer, Macy walked up, followed by a Squirebot butler.

"No, no thank you," Macy was saying, annoyed. "I don't need a jewel-encrusted napkin to wipe my face."

She sighed and turned to her friends. "This place is like being back at the palace. Only, like, ten times worse."

Lance laughed. "If by 'worse' you mean 'fancier,' then you're right."

He raised his arms in the air. "And some more golden slop for Hamletta!" he called out.

Suddenly, they heard a commotion outside. Clay looked over the terrace to see Jestro's monster army storming the golden gates of Auremville! The Evil Mobile rolled along behind them.

Bam! Smash! The Evil Mobile came crashing through, and the terrified Squirebots scattered.

"Grab the gold! Take it all!" Jestro shouted with a gleeful cackle.

"Jestro's attacking!" Clay said. "Hurry, knights! Set up a defense!"

As the knights ran to the mansion's weapons room, the greedy monsters made their way through the streets of Auremville. They grabbed every gold brick, every gold streetlight, every gold bench. They snatched any gold item they could see and tossed it into the mouth of the Evil Mobile.

"Gold! Gold! Gold! Gold!" they chanted.

Burnzie and Sparkks led the monster army down the road leading to the Richmond Mansion.

"Gold! Gold! Gold! Gold!"

The two big monsters crashed through the glass doors and stomped up the stairs, followed by Globlins, Bloblins, and Scurriers. A group of Globlins bounced into the weapons room where the knights were gearing up.

Aaron grabbed a golden sword off the wall—and a Globlin took it right from him! Then the Globlin bounced off.

"They're only interested in getting the gold," Axl said.

"Well, they came to the right place," Aaron said.

The knights were pretty confused. They had never met monsters who were only interested in stealing stuff.

"These monsters are greedy, aren't they?" Macy said.

"Yeah, they do seem pretty wealth-focused," Clay agreed.

"I resent that remark!" Lance called out. He was waving his lance at the monsters, but there were just too many to fight. They knocked him over as they marched back down the stairs.

Lance tumbled into the front hallway—just in time to see monsters carrying his parents away! They were perched in two golden chairs and seemed to have no idea that they were in the middle of a monster attack.

"Isn't the carriage for the spa here a little early?" Goldie wondered.

"Seems so," said Cuthbert. "I'm impressed

with how early they are. And they seem to have an army of staff."

Lance jumped to his feet. "Mom! Dad! They're carrying you off!"

Cutherbert turned to him. "Well, at these prices, we shouldn't expect to walk and dirty our golden shoes!"

"Gold! Gold! Gold! Gold!" the monsters chanted.

The last remaining monsters ran out of the mansion. One of them grabbed Hamletta's golden collar as he went past. Lance watched, helpless, as Jestro's army marched away from the mansion.

Macy, Axl, Aaron, and Clay ran outside.

"Lance, they've taken your parents!" Macy cried.

"It's worse than that," Lance said. "They've taken all my gold!"

CHAPTER 7

"Will I have to live . . . poor?" Lance wailed, burying his face in his hands. "I'll never survive!"

Lance stared to cry. Even Hamletta looked upset.

His fellow knights looked around. Jestro and his greedy monsters had stripped every bit of gold from Auremville.

"You know, money isn't everything, Lance," Macy reminded him.

"Bite your tongue!" Lance cried, jumping to his feet. "How am I supposed to get everyone to do my work for me if I have no money?"

"Have you ever thought that you could simply do your own work?" Clay asked.

Lance shook his head. "*This* is why it's so difficult for me to hang out with commoners!" he said with a sigh.

"Believe me, that goes both ways, bro," Aaron informed him.

"Hey, what we really need to do is get your parents back," Axl said.

"Yes, my parents," Lance said, and then his mind drifted away, to a time not too long ago . . .

Lance was a teenager, and his parents had just told him that he was going away to study at Knights' Academy.

"But why do I have to be a knight?" Lance had protested.

"Because that's what a Richmond is supposed to do," his father replied, sitting in his golden chair.

"But I want to be an actor and a celebrity!" Lance whined. Those things sounded, well, a lot easier than learning how to fight and defend the Realm and stuff like that.

"You're going to be a knight and that's final!" his father insisted, and Lance knew there was no point in arguing anymore. "That's final!" meant that if Lance didn't play along, the money train would stop. No more allowance. No more Squirebots to do his bidding.

So Lance had gone to Knights' Academy, grumbling all the way. Then something funny had happened. Lance discovered that being a knight—especially a handsome, charming knight—had brought him legions of adoring fans. Crowds cheered for him and parents wanted him to take pictures with their babies.

His parents had helped make his dreams come true after all.

Lance glanced down at his new phone, at a photo of his mom and dad. They were smiling and looked happy. What would happen to them in the clutches of Jestro and his monsters?

"Fine, I'll go," Lance said. "But I want to

make it clear that I'm going to save my money, and my parents are just a bonus."

Ava and Robin rolled up in the Fortrex, and the knights climbed on board.

They had monsters to fight and people to save!

CHAPTER 8

Outside Jestro's castle, loud screams could be heard.

If Lance had been there, he might have thought it was his parents in terrible trouble. But it wasn't Goldie and Cuthbert who were screaming.

It was the Globlin they were using as a tennis ball!

"*Aaaaaiiiiieeeeee!*" screeched the Globlin as it soared over a net crudely made from sticks.

Whack! Cuthbert hit the Globlin with his handmade tennis racket. It flew back over the net and then bounced onto the hard granite.

Smack! Goldie hit the Globlin and sent it flying toward Cuthbert.

Lance's parents had no idea that their tennis ball was a monster. Or that they were being held prisoner in a castle. They thought they were at the spa! A fiery, dark, weird spa—but for all they knew, fiery, dark, and weird was the latest fad.

General Magmar walked in to check on his prisoners. Goldie turned when she saw him.

"We'd like a light lunch followed by a sauna and a rub-down," Goldie informed him.

"You'll get boiling tar pits and lava boulders!" snapped General Magmar angrily.

Goldie looked at Cuthbert and nodded. "Hot rock massage? I've always wanted to try that."

General Magmar groaned in frustration and stomped away. He would have to do something about these prisoners!

He marched down to the castle dungeon, where Jestro was admiring a huge gold statue of himself. Piles and piles of gold coins, bars, and other gold objects surrounded him.

"This is so great! I'm literally covered in gold!" Jestro said happily.

The Book of Monsters looked at the statue and frowned. "Yeah, very artsy. Now we got work to do."

Jestro was more interested in gold than doing any evil stuff at the moment.

"Look! I'm so shiny and golden!" he cried, still staring at the statue.

The Book of Monsters turned away from him. "Oh brother. This greed thing is going to his head! And warping his tiny little mind."

General Magmar walked in and saluted.

"Evil Jestro, sir, these prisoners are most annoying and uncooperative," he informed him.

"I didn't want to take prisoners," Jestro said, bouncing a gold coin in his hand. "But they were so, uh, golden, the monsters couldn't resist. Do whatever you want with them."

“Yes sir,” said General Magmar. His eyes narrowed. “I swear by all the evil I know that I . . . will . . . break them.”

The general turned and walked away.

“All these things distract us from finding more books,” The Book of Monsters muttered. Then he yelled to the Bookkeeper. “Hey, rub my chin! I'm thinking to myself.”

While Jestro played with his gold, General Magmar got to work.

First, he gathered Burnzie and Sparkks. They kept an eye on Goldie and Cuthbert. After playing tennis, Lance's parents walked down a long corridor.

“I think the game room is this way, dear,” Goldie told her husband.

Behind them, General Magmar nodded to Burnzie. The big monster sent a sharp, spinning disc flying through the air. It sliced through a rock chandelier hanging down from the ceiling.

Bam! The chandelier came crashing to the ground—just a foot behind Goldie and Cuthbert. It had missed them!

"*Aaaah!*" General Magmar and Burnzie screamed as the spinning disc bounced back and almost sliced through them!

A little while later, General Magmar found Goldie and Cuthbert looking into a pool of bubbling lava. Goldie noticed him and frowned.

"General Manager, I don't think the hot tub is quite hot enough," she said.

"Oh, it will be!" General Magmar promised with an evil cackle. He nodded to Burnzie, who aimed a blast of fire at Lance's parents!

But they had already turned and walked away! The blast missed them and scorched General Magmar. Burnzie gave a shrug of apology.

At dinnertime, Goldie and Cuthbert sat down at a big table to eat. General Magmar placed a bowl of nasty-looking soup in front of Goldie. The soup was making a loud, buzzing sound.

Cuthbert examined it and saw a fly shoot out of it.

"Excuse me, there's a fly in my wife's soup," he told General Magmar.

The general laughed and slammed another bowl down in front of Cuthbert. "There are a THOUSAND flies in your wife's soup! It's fly soup! Now eat it! Eat it all!"

Goldie turned her head away. "Oh, these pretentious chefs! Take it away, take it away!"

"Aaaaaaaaaah!" screamed General Magmar in frustration. His cries echoed throughout the castle.

Goldie and Cuthbert were getting tired of what they thought was bad service. They went to Jestro's gold-filled dungeon to complain.

"Then, when I asked for a fresh mini-umbrella in my drink, your general manager didn't do a thing," Goldie complained.

"Ah, you do know you folks are hostages here, right?" Jestro asked, as The Book of Monsters looked on.

"At these rates, and with this poor level of service, I would say so," said Goldie.

"We are going to the manicure spa," Cuthbert said. "I hope we don't have to make any further complaints."

The Richmonds left the dungeon in a huff.

General Magmar approached Jestro. "They're awful! They complain about everything! They make unreasonable demands. And worse, they're influencing the monsters . . ."

He pointed to Sparkks. He was reclining on a pile of rocks while Burnzie and two Scurriers polished him.

"Everyone around here is completely distracted by greed!" The Book of Monsters complained.

Jestro wasn't listening. He was too busy playing with his gold.

“We could take back the prisoners,” Magmar suggested.

“Yes! And all of this gold and treasure,” said the book. “We have to get back to our core business of being evil.”

Jestro picked up a jester’s hat made out of gold. “But, I love my new hat!” he whined.

He put it on his head. *Wham!* The heavy hat sent him falling to the floor.

The Book of Monsters rolled his eyes. He couldn’t wait to get rid of all this dumb gold!

CHAPTER 9

The knights steered the Fortrex through the countryside, searching for Jestro—and Lance's parents.

Ava motioned for Clay and Macy to join her at the command center. She nodded toward the view screen.

"We've tracked Jestro's position to the Lava Lands," she explained. "Robin hit the Evil Mobile with a tracker—just before they took off with all the gold."

"Obviously we'll have to prepare a mission to rescue Lance's parents," Clay said.

"Meanwhile, Lance is busy preparing for life without coinage," said Macy, nodding toward her fellow knight.

Lance was typing on his tablet, a look of misery on his face.

"I've been forced to sell pictures of myself on KnightBay," he told Dennis, his servant Squirebot. "Me! Forced to be a member of the merchant class."

He handed the tablet to Dennis. The Squirebot examined the smiling photo of Lance that was up for bidding.

"Sir, we're up to three watchers on our auction!" he said happily. Lance just groaned.

Back at the command center, Ava had more to show Clay and Macy.

"I activated the camera on the tracker, and look at this," Ava said. She pressed some keys and a picture of Jestro's lair in the Lava Lands popped up.

"Looks like Jestro has a new castle!" Macy exclaimed.

Clay nodded. "Right. To the training area! So we can prepare to make an assault on Jestro!"

He marched off to gather training equipment. Macy followed him, frowning as she passed Lance.

Sure, we'll rescue Lance's parents, she thought. *But with no help from Lance!*

CHAPTER 10

Back at Jestro's castle, Goldie and Cuthbert were back in the dungeon, angry.

"This is the most poorly run spa I've ever seen!" Cuthbert complained.

"Because this isn't a spa," said a frustrated General Magmar. "It's a terrible monster castle!"

Cuthbert still didn't get it. "Your tar pit facial actually singed my eyebrows!" he yelled.

"Singed?" repeated General Magmar. "They were supposed to *burn!*"

The Richmonds weren't the only ones unhappy at the castle. The monsters were unhappy, too.

"I want more gold!" Burnzie whined like a toddler.

"You can never have enough gold!" Sparkks whined along with him.

The Book of Monsters was out of patience. He turned to Jestro.

"That's it! We're implementing my new plan: Give It All Back," fumed the book. "Right now!"

"Huh?" Jestro said, dropping the gold coins he was admiring.

Jestro might have been an evil jester, but The Book of Monsters was the one calling the shots. Jestro watched, horrified, as the monsters loaded all of the gold into a huge wagon. They lifted up Goldie and Cutherbert and dumped them on top of the gold. Then they pulled the wagon out of the castle and tied it to the back of the Evil Mobile.

The Book of Monsters climbed onto the Evil Mobile and nodded for Jestro to follow him.

"Why are we talking all the gold back?" Jestro moaned.

"Because it's totally ruining our plan for evil domination," The Book of Monsters replied.

The Evil Mobile roared to life and rolled away from the castle, pulling the wagon of gold behind it. The monster army followed behind.

As the Evil Mobile headed toward the villages of Knighton, the Fortrex zoomed toward the Lava Lands.

"I've got Jestro making a run toward the village of Seeling," Ava reported to the team members gathered around her. They watched the blinking tracker on the view screen.

"Seeling? They're the kingdom's leading producer of caulk, sealing, and weatherization products," Robin informed her.

"They might strip this village of its... weather stripping!" Clay cried. "We must defend this place!"

The knights raced for their vehicles. Lance revved up his Turbo Jouster. Clay jumped into his Rumble Blade. Axl climbed into his tank-like Tower Carrier. Macy powered up her Thunder Mace vehicle. Aaron fired up his Aero Striker. The Fortrex door opened up and the knights zoomed out.

They raced down the road, speeding up and down hills. Over the next crest, they saw the Evil Mobile coming toward them.

The Book of Monsters spotted the knights at the same time.

"For the love of monsters!" he yelled, and Burnzie and Sparkks moved ahead, surrounded by lines of Globlins, Bloblins, and Scurriers.

The knights fanned out on the road, blocking the monster army from moving forward.

"Free the Richmonds!" Clay cried as he sped toward the monsters.

"Free my riches!" Lance yelled.

The knights launched into assault mode.

Aaron fired laser blasts from his jet's guns. When the blasts hit the monsters, they exploded in flashes of light and returned to the book.

Axl charged at the monsters in his massive Tower Carrier. Bloblins and Globlins bounced off the vehicle, shrieking.

The laser cannons on Macy's racer roared to life, blasting away more monsters. Clay fired shots from his rocket. Lance's sleek cycle powered forward.

Burnzie pointed at Aaron's Aero Striker. The cannon on the end of his arm opened up and fired at Aaron.

Boom! The blast sent the jet reeling. It nose-dived into the dirt. Aaron ejected and soared through the air on his hover shield, firing at the monsters with his crossbow.

Neeeiiiigh! Lance's cycle transformed into Mecha Horse mode. The vehicle reared up on its hind legs and galloped toward Burnzie.

Vroom! Macy charged toward Sparkks in her racer. The big monster hopped right over her. She skidded into a cart of apples. Then she jumped out of her vehicle, swinging her mace at the one-eyed monster.

Clay zoomed up and ejected from his cockpit, sending his Rumble Blade shooting right at Sparkks. Then he leapt up, sword ready for whatever came his way.

"Knights! We have to get Lance's parents back!" he cried.

"I think Lance wants the gold back, but he'd like his folks to live with Jestro," said Aaron, flying past on his hover shield.

A swarm of chattering, bouncing monsters surrounded the heroes. The knights were fighting a good fight, but they were simply outnumbered.

"Merlok, we need more power!" Lance yelled as a troop of Globlins bounced toward him.

Inside the Fortrex, Ava was furiously typing into the command center keyboard.

"Don't get your chain mail in a bunch!" she replied. The knights could hear her through their helmets. "We're working on it!"

Behind her, the orange holographic image of Merlok 2.0 glowed brightly.

"Yes! Yes!" Merlok cried, as the power surged through him. "Get ready for a NEXO Power!"

CHAPTER 11

As Merlok powered up the download, the knights kept battling monsters.

Macy faced Sparkks and spun around, building up momentum for her attack.

Whack! She smacked him with her mace, and the big, one-eyed monster fell backward. He knocked into a sealant vendor's wagon, sending a box of coins scattering across the road.

At the sight of the shiny coins, the greedy monsters went nuts!

"Gold! Gold! Gold! Gold!" they chanted as they scrambled over one another—and pushed aside the knights—to pick up the fallen gold.

"They're completely money crazy," said Clay, waving his sword at a passing Globlin.

"Huh?" said Macy, pushing a Scurrier away with her power mace. "Remind you of anyone?"

Just then, the helmet of every knight began to glow and beep. Merlok 2.0 was ready for the download. Clay, Macy, Axl, Aaron, and Lance raised their shields toward the sky.

"Merlok!" Lance cried. "NEXOOO KNIGHTS!"

A glowing holographic creature appeared—it had a body like a lion and the face and wings of an eagle. The creature was a symbol of the NEXO Power they were about to download.

"NEXO Power: Griffin of Graciousness!" Merlok 2.0 announced.

Lance's shield glowed brightly as it downloaded the NEXO Power. The energy spread throughout his armor and into his lance.

The other knights powered up, too. Aaron's crossbow glowed with the energy. So did

Clay's sword, Macy's mace, and Axl's double-sided axe.

Powered by the Griffin of Graciousness, the knights tore like tornadoes through the army of monsters.

"*Hyah!*" With one whack of Macy's mace, six Globlins dissolved into a purple cloud. It streamed back into The Book of Monsters.

Slash! Just one blow from Clay's sword sent eight Bloblins back to the book.

Bam! Wham! Smack! In seconds, the knights had dissolved more than half of the monsters.

From his perch in the Evil Mobile, Jestro's eyes grew wide with fear.

"Now what?" he asked The Book of Monsters.

"We gotta make a deal!" the book said.

Jestro shook his head. "No way!"

"We got no choice," said the book. He shouted out to the knights. "Hey, hold on! We don't want to fight. We want to make a deal!"

The knights stopped fighting and looked at each other, confused.

"What did he say?" Macy asked.

"He says they want to make a deal," Clay replied, but he didn't sound like he believed it.

"Look, we just want to give you Lance's parents back," Jestro said, and The Book of Monsters gave him a look. "Oh, and all the gold."

"What?" Macy still couldn't believe what she was hearing.

"That actually sounds like a win-win," said Aaron.

"No deal!" Lance called back. "We'll take the gold and you can keep my parents."

Jestro frowned and turned to The Book of Monsters. "What?"

"Sounds like some kind of reverse psychology trick," the book guessed. "We gotta make some new outrageous demands of our own! That's how these things work."

Jestro nodded. "Right," he said. Then he

shouted back to the knights again. "No deal! You take the gold, the crazy rich people, and we want . . ."

He looked around. There wasn't much in the town of Seeling except for stuff you could use to seal things with. Then he spotted something.

"We want a bunch of weather-proof caulk for some, uh, home renovation projects!" Jestro finished.

"What?" asked The Book of Monsters.

Jestro put a hand over his mouth. "We gotta weather-seal the new hot tub," he reminded the book in a low voice.

The Book of Monsters nodded. "Ah, good thinking."

Lance was still considering the offer.

"Hmm," he said. "My parents for a tube of sealant . . ."

Clay looked at him. "Really? Do you actually have to think about it?"

Macy didn't give him a chance to back down.

"Deal!" she shouted.

"Burnzie! Sparkks!" Jestro cried. The two big monsters placed Goldie and Cuthbert in the middle of the square. Lance walked toward them, holding the giant tube of caulk. Lance tossed the tube to the monsters, and they let go of Lance's parents.

Goldie and Cuthbert frowned and they walked away from the Evil Mobile.

"Shall we leave them a bad review online?" Cuthbert asked.

"Absolutely!" agreed Goldie. "That was the worst spa vacation ever!"

CHAPTER 12

Back in Auremville, Lance and the other knights stood among the piles of returned gold in the grand hall of the Richmond Mansion. Goldie and Cuthbert happily perched in their golden chairs and smiled at everyone.

"Son, we are happy you're a knight," his father said. "And you have good taste in friends."

"What we're trying to say, Lancelot, is that it's good to be home," said Goldie.

"Well, mother, I didn't think I'd say this, but it's good to have you home," Lance said. "And this whole knight thing has been growing on me . . . sort of."

Macy elbowed Clay and smiled.

"Now be a good boy and count all the money," Goldie told him.

Lance sighed. "Fine. I'll do the servant's chores, just this once."

He looked around the room. There were stacks of coins, piles of coins, mountains of coins, everywhere he looked. He sighed again and started counting.

"One . . . two . . . three . . . four . . ."

Ava walked up to him. "What are you doing?" she asked.

"I'm counting," Lance replied.

"Seems pretty labor-intensive," Ava said with a sly grin on her face.

"It is," Lance said. "Say, could I pay you to count all these coins?"

"Sure," Ava said, holding out her hand. Lance dropped some coins into it. Ava pocketed the coins and started typing on her tablet.

"Average weight of one coin," she said,

while she typed. "Circumference of said coin . . . total area of all coins . . . volume of area . . ."

She stopped typing and looked up. "You have one million, six hundred and eighty-five thousand, two hundred and twelve coins here."

Lance looked surprised. "Really? How did you do that?"

"It's called math," Ava replied. "Try it sometime."

Lance brightened. "Better yet, I'll pay Dennis to do some math for me." He ran off to find his favorite Squirebot. "Dennis? Dennis!"

"You can always 'count' on Lance," Ava said, and then she groaned at her own joke. "I'm letting my cleverness go to my head!"

CHAPTER 13

Back at Jestro's castle, the evil jester sat on his throne, frowning. Nearby, General Magmar worked with Burnzie and Sparkks to seal the bubbling hot tub. Burnzie squirted the caulk out of the giant tube.

"I'm kind of missing my huge piles of gold," Jestro said with a sigh as he looked around.

"Hey, you still got a golden statue of yourself," The Book of Monsters reminded him. "That's quite a conversation starter. Besides, you need to be focused on the big picture: finding more evil books!"

Burnzie jumped on the big tube to get out more caulk.

Squish! It squirted onto Sparkks. The big monster tried to wipe it off, and his hand got stuck to his own leg!

"Books, books, books," complained Jestro. "What am I, a librarian?"

"Look, when we find the magic number of evil books, well . . . then some real nastiness can be unleashed," The Book of Monsters said, his orange eyes burning at the thought.

Burnzie pulled on Sparkks' arm—and he got stuck to Sparkks! General Magmar tried to pull them apart—and he got stuck to them!

"Real nastiness?" Jestro asked, perking up.

"Trust me, joke-boy," said The Book of Monsters, with a grin even more evil than usual. "You ain't seen nothing yet!"